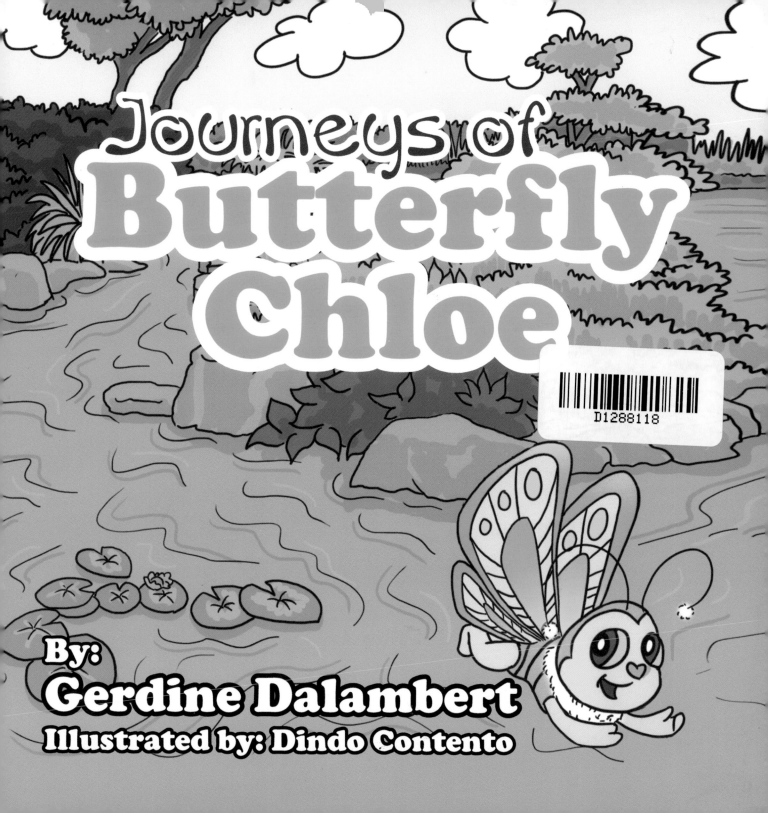

Journeys of Butterfly Chloe

By:
Gerdine Dalambert
Illustrated by: Dindo Contento

To order additional copies of this book, contact:
Xlibris Corporation
1-888-795-4274
www.Xlibris.com
Orders@Xlibris.com

Dedication

This book is written for the children
of the world.

May all your dreams become reality and all your wishes
come true.

In loving memory of

Marie Germaine Pierre Dalambert

There once was an egg, a tiny green egg that lived in a leaf. Its wiggle and jiggle makes everyone giggle.

1

Tic, Tack, uh oh... a crack. Push, push, slide, squish, and swoosh. Don't blink or you will miss the exciting bliss.

A cute little critter, oh my! It's a caterpillar. The caterpillar has many legs; it came from a tiny green egg. The caterpillar worked very hard, you see. It was getting very hungry.

Caterpillars eat their egg shells; it tastes like cookies, Yummy! They like Milkweed too. Munch, crunch, crunch, munch. Caterpillars love milkweed, indeed.

3

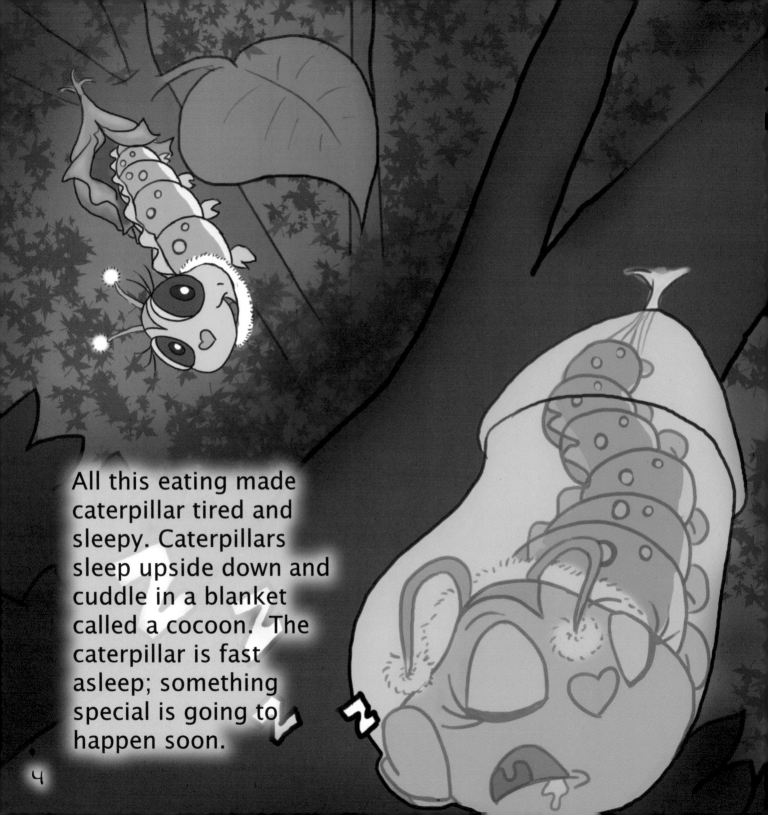

All this eating made caterpillar tired and sleepy. Caterpillars sleep upside down and cuddle in a blanket called a cocoon. The caterpillar is fast asleep; something special is going to happen soon.

4

Time to wake up! Ugh, wonk, pop, and clop. "I can do it," said the little butterfly. Look at the cocoon. Flop, growl, and drop. The butterfly yelled, "I am doing it." It is really tough to get out of this cocoon stuff.

How pretty; it's a butterfly! The pretty butterfly came from the cute caterpillar, which came from a tiny green egg. She rubs the sleep that covered her eyes. The butterfly does not know how to fly.

She is trying and trying; she does not want to start crying.

Her feet flutter as she spread her yellow wings that sing. Wow, there she goes, she is flying.

She flies low, she flies high; we can't deny.

6

She sees an orange perfect for lunch; butterfly leaps to the sweet juice. Orange and watermelon are her favorite fruits. The animals stared at her in awe; she drinks with a mouth that looks like a straw.

Butterfly flew high with glee, amazed at all she could see. Flying low, butterfly did not know, the water in the pond showed her face in the space below. Butterfly hid, the picture made her timid. Then she said "Is that me, I see?".

The water tickled her feet as she skid. She laughed and flew to look for something new.

The loudest noise she could ever hear, thunder and rain drops are here.

11

Butterfly flew, shaking in fear. She could not stop the tears; she is alone, cold with no blanket to hold. Butterfly said, "A hole in the tree, a safe place for me, I see. Yippee!"

She flew as fast as she could, she felt her heart beating out loud. It sounded like the thunder from the cloud.

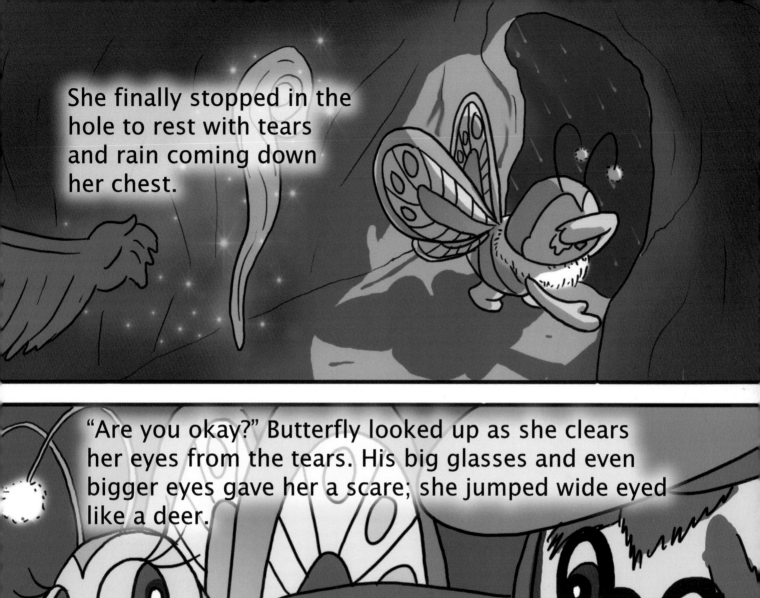

She finally stopped in the hole to rest with tears and rain coming down her chest.

"Are you okay?" Butterfly looked up as she clears her eyes from the tears. His big glasses and even bigger eyes gave her a scare; she jumped wide eyed like a deer.

13

"Who are you?" she begged. I am named Mr. Knowledge; I am an owl who knows it all. "Who am I?" replied butterfly.

You are butterfly Chloe. Chloe smiled looking at her face in his big glasses. "Who made me?" asked Chloe.

Owl went on saying, "Your purpose is to discover all your heart desire. Don't be afraid, the One who made you is in you, you're not alone.

Mr. Knowledge smiled and said,
"The One who made you, made me,
and everything you see.

15

The two of you are one; your journey is far from done. Chloe smiles, "Thank you Mr. Knowledge. I am glad to be me." Chloe fell fast asleep... dreaming of all the wonderful things she'll explore and see.

The end

Color your own butterfly!

18

Discoveries coming soon:

Chloe meets Brian Bee in the city
Chloe meets Carlos the can't ant
Chloe meets scared Suzy Spider

The illustrations are from
Brandon, Dylan and Guedalia Dalambert

CPSIA information can be obtained
at www.ICGtesting.com
Printed in the USA
258453LV00002B